On a Hill

Written by
Karen Hoenecke

Illustrated by
Peggy M. Tagel

On a hill, there is a farm.

In the pond, there is a plant.

On the plant, there is a flower.

In the flower, there is a seed.

Along comes a bird chirping tweet! tweet! tweet!

And that is the end of the tiny little seed.